Scholastic Publications Ltd.,
10 Earlham Street, London WC2H 9RX, UK

Scholastic Inc.,
730 Broadway, New York, NY 10003, USA

Scholastic Tab Publications Ltd.,
123 Newkirk Road, Richmond Hill,
Ontario L4C 3G5, Canada

Ashton Scholastic Pty. Ltd.,
P O Box 579, Gosford, New South Wales,
Australia

Ashton Scholastic Ltd.,
165 Marua Road, Panmure, Auckland 6,
New Zealand

First published by Scholastic Publications Limited, 1988
Reprinted 1988
Text copyright © John Cunliffe, 1988
Illustrations copyright © Scholastic Publications Limited and
Woodland Animations Limited, 1988

ISBN 0 590 70907 0

Made and printed in Hong Kong
Typeset in Times Roman by AKM Associates (UK) Ltd,
Ajmal House, Hayes Road, Southall, London

Postman Pat
Goes to Town

Story by **John Cunliffe** *Pictures by* **Joan Hickson**
From the original Television designs by **Ivor Wood**

Hippo Books
in association with André Deutsch

"What's all this," said Mrs Goggins, "about you going to London?"

"Oh, it's true enough," said Pat. "I'll be down there for a week – at the end of May."

"Whatever for, Pat? Isn't Greendale good enough for you?"

"My goodness," Pat laughed, "Greendale's certainly good enough for me. There's no better place in all the world. But I have to go to London, just for a week. There was a letter from Pencaster, from the boss. It's all part of this new training scheme. The country postmen have to spend a week in town, and the town postmen have to spend a week in the country."

"Funny idea," said Mrs Goggins. "What a muddle there'll be. I don't know who will get the most mixed up."

"Oh, I don't know," said Pat. "It might be fun."

"Well, they'd better not send *me* to London, that's all I can say," said Mrs Goggins. "I'm staying here and that's that."

"You don't know what you might be missing," said Pat.

"Not much," said Mrs Goggins. "Aunt
Lucy went to London, once, and she lost
her purse."

9

"Your aunt Lucy once lost a cow, in Greendale," said Pat, laughing. "And that was nobody's fault but her own!"

"Oh! Goodness me, Pat! I'd quite forgotten that!"

"If she could lose a cow she could lose anything," said Pat.

"And nobody ever knew how it managed to turn up in the Reverend Timms' garden," said Mrs Goggins.

"He was very nice about it," said Pat, "considering that it ate a row of his lettuces. Well, well, I'd better be off with these letters. Cheerio!"

And Pat was on his way.

The weeks went by, and spring came to
Greendale. Then it was time for Pat to go
to London. He was so excited! Sara and
Julian saw him off at Pencaster station.

The big inter-city train rumbled down the
track from Carlisle, and whisked Pat
away. Away it took him, whizzing along
at great speed. Past farms, and fields, and
motorways, and churches, and villages,
and towns, and factories, and canals, and
houses, and schools, and more houses,
and trees, and hills, and valleys, and on,
and on, and on!

Pat looked out of the window.

"Bless me," he said to himself. "What a big place the world is. What a lot of places there are! And what a lot of people!"

And then he saw a postman's van, just like his own, going along a road. "And they all get letters," said Pat. "There must be hundreds and hundreds of postmen. I wonder if any of them have a cat like Jess?"

A snack trolley came along the train.
Pat had a cup of coffee, a bag of crisps,
and an apple pie. Then he had a snooze.
And soon it was, "Tickets, please!"

There were fewer fields outside, and more and more houses and factories. The speakers crackled. A voice said, "We will be arriving at Euston in ten minutes' time. Thank you for travelling with inter-city. Please make sure you have left nothing on the train. Thank you."

When Pat saw the crowds at Euston, he almost got back on the train to go home to Greendale! There were thousands of people, and they all seemed to be in a hurry. Pat felt dizzy. He just stood in the middle of it all, and let the people swirl around him.

What should he do now?
Which way should he go? He saw a man,
holding a piece of card in front of him.
What did it say?

POST OFFICE
STAFF
MEETING
POINT

Post office? Where? Oh! STAFF. Perhaps this man was . . . ? Pat went up to him.

"Excuse me. Are you from the Post Office? Are you . . ."

"That's right, guv. Hang on a mo . . . You on my list . . . ? Name?"

"Um . . . er . . . Pat."

"Pat who?"

"Pat Clifton. From Greendale."

"Gotcher. Hang on a jiffy, mate. We'll soon get the show on the road. We've got another six to collect."

The man talked so fast, and in such a funny way, that Pat hardly knew what he was saying. But he had a Post Office badge on his coat, just like Pat's, so it must be all right. And, as they stood there, six more lost-looking postmen came and gathered round the man with the card, and the man ticked off their names on his list. They all, Pat thought, talked in a funny way, and one of them wore a kilt.

"Na' then," said the man with the card, "we're all here. My name's Fred. Got the minibus round the back, and I'll run you down to the canteen for a cuppa', then you'll be seeing the gaffer. Okay?"

And he was off at a trot before anyone could say a word, with all seven postmen hurrying after him.

There was a Post Office minibus in the
goods yard. Fred flung the doors open,
and they all got in.

They were off at speed through the streets
of London, hanging on for dear life. Fred
seemed to think he was on a race-track.
Black taxis and big red London buses
zoomed past them, and Fred shouted
jokes at the drivers through his open
window. What a noisy, smelly place
London was!

There were more surprises when they arrived at the Post Office building. They went into a huge dining-hall, where hundreds of people were having meals and drinks.

"Just look!" said Pat. "There are more post*women* than post*men*."

"And they're a great bunch!" said Fred.

"We could do with a few of them in Pencaster," said Pat.

There were so many things to do and see in London that Pat was glad when Fred said, "Right, mates. Knocking-off time. I'll run you round to the hotel."

They were all so tired that they slept soundly, even though the London refuse collectors seemed to start emptying the bins in the middle of the night.

The next day, Fred came for them all very early, and took them racing off in the minibus.

"Time to do some work, now!" shouted Fred, cheerfully. He dropped each of them at a different post office.

"We'll get lost!" said Pat.

"Don't worry," said Fred. "You'll be going out with somebody who knows the ropes. You'll not be on your own."

"I wish I had Jess and my van with me," thought Pat.

But when Pat met the person he was working with for the day, he forgot all about Jess and his van.

"This is Val," said Fred. "She'll look after you. You'll have a good laugh with Val. Ta ra!"

With a big smile, Val nearly shook Pat's hand off. She seemed to find everything a big joke.

"Hi!" she said. "Good to see ya! Welcome to Happy Hampstead! I hope you're good on hills? We got plenty hills in Hampstead. Let's go to it, Pat!"

There were more letters in the sorting-office than Pat had ever seen all at once. It seemed as if all the world's letters had arrived in Hampstead that day.

"It's nothing," said Val. "We'll soon shift this lot."

Pat wasn't much help with the sorting, as he didn't know the names of the streets on their walk, or the order they should come in. But Val sorted them at an amazing speed.

"I'm not much of a help, am I?" said Pat.

"You'll be a great help," said Val. "You can carry the parcels. I hate them blessed parcels, I really do."

Off they went, into the hills of Hampstead.
In and out of shops, and offices.
Up stairs and down stairs in the flats,
and down again to basements, half
under the ground. In and out of garden
gates. Down back alleys, into yards, and
in and out of squares.

Dogs barked and snapped at them.
People pushed by them in their hurry.
Cars, and taxis, and buses, and lorries
made a roaring and a smell all day.

Pat's legs began to ache. His back began to ache. He thought again of his van, with Jess sitting in his basket. But Val kept him smiling. She told him stories about the people and the places they saw. She told him about her home in Jamaica. She sang Jamaican songs. She made him forget how tired he was.

They called at the church. It made Pat
think of Greendale Church. He half
expected to see the Reverend Timms
come smiling out to meet them. But it
was a young man with red hair who met
them at the door, and he was carrying a
guitar!

Their bags were empty at last.

"Thank goodness," said Pat.

"Oh, that's just the beginning," said Val. "We have to go back for another lot, now!"

She took pity on Pat. "But we'll stop for a coffee, first," she said.

"Great!" said Pat.

While they were doing their second delivery, Pat told Val all about Greendale. Her eyes grew big and round.

"Say, I'd sure like to come and see it."

"Why don't you?" said Pat. "I've come to see you. You come to see me in my place."

"I'll have to ask the boss," said Val.

As the week went on, Pat could be more help to Val. He began to know his way about.

"I'll be sorry to see you go," she said.

"You're just getting to be useful."

On Wednesday, after their work was done, Val took Pat to meet her family. Val's husband cooked a Jamaican meal. Pat loved it.

"You'll have to give me the recipe," he said. "I'll make some of this for Sara and Julian."

On Thursday, Pat took them all for a meal at a Chinese restaurant.

And on Friday, Val's friend, Dipali,
made them a hot curry. Then they went
to hear a steel band at the church hall.

41

Saturday was a free day, when all the
visiting postmen and postwomen could
go and see the sights of London. Pat saw
Buckingham Palace, the Tower of
London, Piccadilly Circus, and London
Zoo. Pat had lunch at Harrods. He sent
postcards to Sara and Julian, and bought
presents for them. Then it was time to
pack up and catch the tube to Euston
station.

Fred and Val and lots of other Post Office people came to see them off. Everyone shook hands, and said, "Thanks for a great week," and Val promised to come and see Pat in Greendale.

The train soon got up speed. There was more and more green between the houses and factories. Pat saw a grassy hill, with trees on the top and sheep all over it. Then he knew how much he had missed Greendale. But he was on his way home, now. He smiled, and closed his eyes, and went to sleep.

And it didn't seem long before the voice on the speakers was saying,

"We are now arriving at Pencaster. All change for trains to Windermere — Pencaster!" and Pat was getting sleepily out on to the windy platform of Pencaster station, and giving Sara and Julian a hug. They asked him so many questions about his week in London that he felt almost as muddled as the day he arrived at Euston and stood in the middle of the great crowd of people.

"I'll tell you all about it," he said, "*tomorrow*."

Ted was waiting in his Landrover, and he drove them home to Greendale.

"It's good to be back," said Pat.

But the next Saturday afternoon, he took Sara and Julian to Lancaster for a Chinese meal.